Zuri's Day of Pranks

Written by Tanisha Chambers
Illustrated by Visnja Pokorni

Printed in the United States of America
First Printing, 2018
ISBN-13:
978-1719250900

www.Tanishachambers.com

This book belongs to:

_____

Zuri sat on a mat
and played with her cat
in a hat.

5

Zuri ran and told that.

"Mommy, Mommy!" Zuri yelled.
"My brothers called me a brat!"

Zuri's mommy said, "Please stop chat."

Then Zuri decided she was going to play a trick on them.

Zuri went and got some tooth paste

Love

She told her mommy her plans.

Zuri and her mommy needed two things:
toothpaste and Oreos.

So they got some
Oreos out of the
kitchen cabinet,
scrapped the white
cream off,
and put tooth paste
all inside instead.

10

Zuri was so thankful
for her mommy's help.

"This will be the
best trick ever!"
Zuri said as she smiled
and got a plate and
placed it on the table.

11

Just like that, her brothers walked over
and picked up a cookie, only to realize
when they took a bite,
they had tooth paste all in their mouth.

Zuri laughed and said,
"That will teach you guys to call me a brat!"

Zuri played with her cat Kurly,
only to run up the stairs and hear a splash

14

She looked down
and saw a red ballon

Zuri heard giggles
come from a room

15

She continued to run up the steps
and saw her brothers.

They looked at her and said,
"That will teach you
to play a trick like that."

Zuri laughed and took her hand
and smacked them only for
them to stumble
and both fall on their back

17

Zuri ran and sat in her room.

"that will teach them
to play with me like that."

Zuri played with
brown bear Claire
and a pair of deer.

Only to learn
she doesn't care.

19

Zuri threw her deer
up in the air,
only for them to hit her
in her hair.

"Ouch!"
Zuri screamed.
As tears began to drip
down her face.

Zuri sat on her bed
with lots of grace,
not wanting
her thoughts to be
all over the place.

So she decided to take a nap

23

Only to wake up
to lipstick all over her face

24

Zuri ran
to her brother's room,
only to say sorry
and wave her white flag

25

Zuri hugged her brothers and told them that she was finished playing tricks on them.

But Zuri knew that was only until tomorrow!

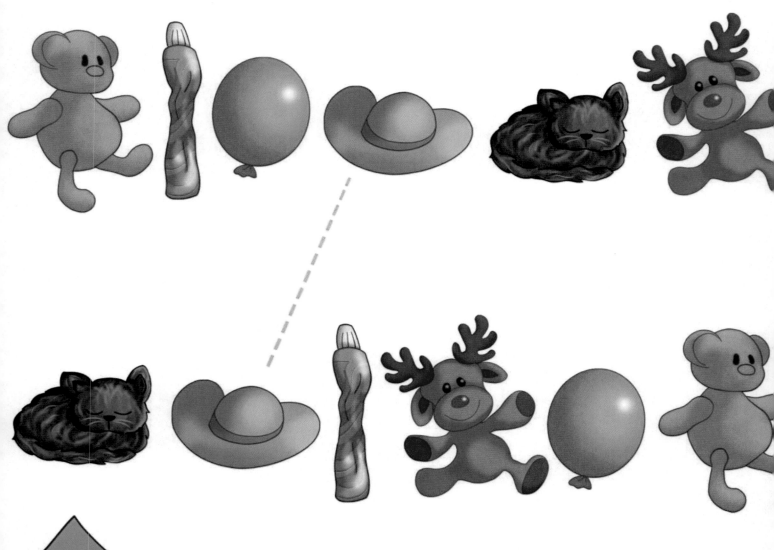

Draw lines between same items!

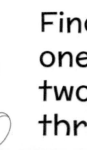

Find and color:
one cat and one hat
two dears
three baloons!

28

Made in the USA
Middletown, DE
05 October 2021